THE WAY WE LIVE NOW

THE WAY WE LIVE NOW

Susan Sontag

Howard Hodgkin

The Noonday Press
Farrar, Straus & Giroux
New York

All royalties from this edition of
The Way We Live Now are being given
to AIDS charities in the United Kingdom
and the United States

THE WAY WE LIVE NOW

AT FIRST HE WAS just losing weight, he felt only a little ill, Max said to Ellen, and he didn't call for an appointment with his doctor, according to Greg, because he was managing to keep on working at more or less the same rhythm, but he did stop smoking, Tanya pointed out, which suggests he was frightened, but also that he wanted, even more than he knew, to be healthy, or healthier, or maybe just to gain back a few pounds, said Orson, for he told her, Tanya went on, that he expected to be climbing the walls (isn't that what people say?) and found, to his surprise, that he didn't miss cigarettes at all and revelled in the sensation of his lungs being ache-free for the first time in years. But did he have a good doctor, Stephen wanted to know, since it would have been crazy not to go for a checkup after the pressure was off and he was back from the conference in Helsinki, even if by then he was feeling better. And he said, to Frank, that he would go, even though he was indeed frightened, as he admitted to Jan, but who wouldn't be frightened now, though, odd as that might seem, he hadn't been worrying until recently, he avowed to Quentin, it was only in the last six months that he had the metallic taste of panic in his mouth, because becoming seriously ill was exaggerating now, Quentin said, smiling. Right, said Kate, so if I want to bring him a whole raft of stuff, besides chocolate and licorice, what else. Jelly beans, Quentin said.

He didn't want to be alone, according to Paolo, and lots of people came in the first week, and the Jamaican nurse said there were other patients on the floor who would be glad to have the surplus flowers, and people weren't afraid to visit, it wasn't like the old days, as Kate pointed out to Aileen, they're not even segregated in the hospital any more, as Hilda observed, there's nothing on the door of his room warning visitors of the possibility of contagion, as there was a few years ago; in fact, he's in a double room and, as he told Orson, the old guy on the far side of the curtain (who's clearly on the way out, said Stephen) doesn't even have the disease, so, as Kate went on, you really should go and see him, he'd be happy to see you, he likes having people visit, you aren't not going because you're afraid, are you. Of course not, Aileen said, but I don't know what to say, I think I'll feel awkward, which he's bound to notice, and that will make him feel worse, so I won't be doing him any good, will I. But he won't notice anything, Kate said, patting Aileen's hand, it's not like that, it's not the way you imagine, he's not judging people or wondering about their motives, he's just happy to see his friends. But I never was really a friend of his, Aileen said, you're a friend, he's always liked you, you told me he talks about Nora with you, I know he likes me, he's even attracted to me, but he respects you. But, according to Wesley, the reason Aileen was so stingy with her visits was that she could never have him to herself, there were always others there already and by the time they left still others had arrived, she'd been in love with him for years, and I can understand, said Donny, that Aileen should feel bitter that if there could have been a woman friend he did more than occasionally bed, a woman he really loved, and my God, Victor said, who had known him in those years, he was crazy about Nora, what a heartrending couple they were, two surly angels, then it couldn't have been she.

And when some of the friends, the ones who came every day, waylaid the doctor in the corridor, Stephen was the one who asked the most informed questions, who'd been keeping up not just with the stories that appeared several times a week in the *Times* (which Greg confessed to have stopped reading, unable to stand it any more) but with articles in the medical journals published here and in England and France, and who knew socially one of the principal doctors in Paris who was doing some much-publicized research on the disease, but his doctor said little more than that the pneumonia was not life-threatening, the fever was subsiding, of course he was still weak but he was responding well to the antibiotics, that he'd have to complete his stay in the hospital, which entailed a minimum of twenty-one days on the I.V., before she could start him on the new drug, for she was optimistic about the possibility of getting him into the protocol; and when Victor said that if he had so much trouble eating (he'd say to everyone, when they coaxed him to eat some of the hospital meals, that food didn't taste right, that he had a funny metallic taste in his mouth) it couldn't be good that friends were bringing him all that chocolate, the doctor just smiled and said that in these cases the patient's morale was also an important factor, and if chocolate made him feel better she saw no harm in it, which worried Stephen, as Stephen said later to Donny, because they wanted to believe in the promises and taboos of today's high-tech medicine but here this reassuringly curt and silver-haired specialist in the disease, someone quoted frequently in the papers, was talking like some oldfangled country G.P. who tells the family that tea with honey or chicken soup may do as much for the patient as penicillin, which might mean, as Max said, that they were just going through the motions of treating him, that they were not sure about what to do, or rather, as Xavier interjected, that they didn't know what the hell they were doing, that the truth, the real truth, as Hilda said, upping the ante, was that they didn't, the doctors, really have any hope.

Oh, no, said Lewis, I can't stand it, wait a minute, I can't believe it, are you sure, I mean are they sure, have they done all the tests, it's getting so when the phone rings I'm scared to answer because I think it will be someone telling me someone else is ill; but did Lewis really not know until yesterday, Robert said testily, I find that hard to believe, everybody is talking about it, it seems impossible that someone wouldn't have called Lewis; and perhaps Lewis did know, was for some reason pretending not to know already, because, Jan recalled, didn't Lewis say something months ago to Greg, and not only to Greg, about his not looking well, losing weight, and being worried about him and wishing he'd see a doctor, so it couldn't come as a total surprise. Well, everybody is worried about everybody now, said Betsy, that seems to be the way we live, the way we live now. And, after all, they were once very close, doesn't Lewis still have the keys to his apartment, you know the way you let someone keep the keys after you've broken up, only a little because you hope the person might just saunter in, drunk or high, late some evening, but mainly because it's wise to have a few sets of keys strewn around town, if you live alone, at the top of a former commercial building that, pretentious as it is, will never acquire a doorman or even a resident superintendent, someone whom you can call on for the keys late one night if you find you've lost yours or have locked yourself out. Who else has keys, Tanya inquired, I was thinking somebody might drop by tomorrow before coming to the hospital and bring some treasures, because the other day, Ira said, he was complaining about how dreary the hospital room was, and how it was like being locked up in a motel room, which got everybody started telling funny stories about motel rooms they'd known, and at Ursula's story, about the Luxury Budget Inn in Schenectady, there was an uproar of laughter around his bed, while he watched them in silence, eyes bright with fever, all the while, as Victor recalled, gobbling that damned chocolate. But, according to Jan, whom Lewis's keys enabled to tour the swank of his bachelor lair with an eye to bringing over some art consolation to brighten up the hospital room, the Byzantine icon wasn't on the wall over his bed, and that was a puzzle until Orson remembered that he'd recounted without seeming upset (this disputed by Greg) that the boy he'd recently gotten rid of had stolen it, along with four of the *maki-e* lacquer boxes, as if these were objects as easy to sell on the street as a TV or a stereo. But he's always been very generous, Kate said quietly, and though he loves beautiful things isn't really attached to them, to things, as Orson said, which is unusual in a collector, as Frank commented, and when Kate shuddered and tears sprang to her eyes and Orson inquired anxiously if he, Orson, had said something wrong, she pointed out that they'd begun talking about him in a retrospective mode, summing up what he was like, what made them fond of him, as if he were finished, completed, already a part of the past.

Perhaps he was getting tired of having so many visitors, said Robert, who was, as Ellen couldn't help mentioning, someone who had come only twice and was probably looking for a reason not to be in regular attendance, but there could be no doubt, according to Ursula, that his spirits had dipped, not that there was any discouraging news from the doctors, and he seemed now to prefer being alone a few hours of the day; and he told Donny that he'd begun keeping a diary for the first time in his life, because he wanted to record the course of his mental reactions to this astonishing turn of events, to do something parallel to what the doctors were doing, who came every morning and conferred at his bedside about his body, and that perhaps it wasn't so important what he wrote in it, which amounted, as he said wryly to Quentin, to little more than the usual banalities about terror and amazement that this was happening to him, to him also, plus the usual remorseful assessments of his past life, his pardonable superficialities, capped by resolves to live better, more deeply, more in touch with his work and his friends, and not to care so passionately about what people thought of him, interspersed with admonitions to himself that in this situation his will to live counted more than anything else and that if he really wanted to live, and trusted life, and liked himself well enough (down, ol' debbil Thanatos!), he *would* live, he would be an exception; but perhaps all this, as Quentin ruminated, talking on the phone to Kate, wasn't the

point, the point was that by the very keeping of the diary he was accumulating something to reread one day, slyly staking out his claim to a future time, in which the diary would be an object, a relic, in which he might not actually reread it, because he would want to have put this ordeal behind him, but the diary would be there in the drawer of his stupendous Majorelle desk, and he could already, he did actually say to Quentin one late sunny afternoon, propped up in the hospital bed, with the stain of chocolate framing one corner of a heartbreaking smile, see himself in the penthouse, the October sun streaming through those clear windows instead of this streaked one, and the diary, the pathetic diary, safe inside the drawer

It doesn't matter about the treatment's side effects, Stephen said (when talking to Max), I don't know why you're so worried about that, every strong treatment has some dangerous side effects, it's inevitable, you mean otherwise the treatment wouldn't be effective, Hilda interjected, and anyway, Stephen went on doggedly, just because there *are* side effects it doesn't mean he has to get them, or all of them, each one, or even some of them. That's just a list of all the possible things that could go wrong, because the doctors have to cover themselves, so they make up a worst-case scenario, but isn't what's happening to him, and to so many other people, Tanya interrupted, a worst-case scenario, a catastrophe no one could have imagined, it's too cruel, and isn't everything a side effect, quipped Ira, even *we* are all side effects, but we're not bad side effects, Frank said, he likes having his friends around, and we're helping each other, too; because his illness sticks us all in the same glue, mused Xavier, and, whatever the jealousies and grievances from the past that have made us wary and cranky with each other, when something like this happens (the sky is falling, the sky is falling!) you understand what's really important. I agree, Chicken Little, he is reported to have said. But don't you think, Quentin observed to Max, that being as close to him as we are, making time to drop by the hospital every day, is a way of our trying to define ourselves more firmly and irrevocably as the well, those who aren't ill, who aren't going to fall ill, as if what's happened to him couldn't happen to us, when in fact the chances are that before long one of us will end up where he is, which is probably what he felt when he was one of the cohort visiting Zack in the spring (you never knew Zack, did you?), and, according to Clarice, Zack's widow, he didn't come very often, he said he hated hospitals, and didn't feel he was doing Zack any good, that Zack would see on his face how uncomfortable he was. Oh, he was one of those, Aileen said. A coward. Like me.

And after he was sent home from the hospital, and Quentin had volunteered to move in and was cooking meals and taking telephone messages and keeping the mother in Mississippi informed, well, mainly keeping her from flying to New York and heaping her grief on her son and confusing the household routine with her oppressive ministrations, he was able to work an hour or two in his study, on days he didn't insist on going out, for a meal or a movie, which tired him. He seemed optimistic, Kate thought, his appetite was good, and what he said, Orson reported, was that he agreed when Stephen advised him that the main thing was to keep in shape, he was a fighter, right, he wouldn't be who he was if he weren't, and was he ready for the big fight, Stephen asked rhetorically (as Max told it to Donny), and he said you bet, and Stephen added it could be a lot worse, you could have gotten the disease two years ago, but now so many scientists are working on it, the American team and the French team, everyone bucking for that Nobel Prize a few years down the road, that all you have to do is stay healthy for another year or two and then there will be good treatment, real treatment. Yes, he said, Stephen said, my timing is good. And Betsy, who had been climbing on and rolling off macrobiotic diets for a decade, came up with a Japanese specialist she wanted him to see but thank God, Donny reported, he'd had the sense to refuse, but he did agree to see Victor's visualization therapist, although what could one possibly visualize, said Hilda, when the point of visualizing disease was to see it as an entity with contours, borders, here rather than there, something limited, something you were the host of, in the sense that you could disinvite the disease, while this was so total; or would be, Max said. But the main thing, said Greg, was to see that he didn't go the macrobiotic route, which might be harmless for plump Betsy but could only be devastating for him, lean as he'd always been, with all the cigarettes and other appetite-suppressing chemicals he'd been welcoming into his body for years; and now was hardly the time, as Stephen pointed out, to be worried about cleaning up his act, and eliminating the chemical additives and other pollutants that we're all blithely or not so blithely feasting on, blithely since we're healthy, healthy as we can be; so far, Ira said. Meat and potatoes is what I'd be happy to see him eating, Ursula said wistfully. And spaghetti and clam sauce, Greg added. And thick cholesterol-rich omelettes with smoked mozzarella, suggested Yvonne, who had flown from London for the weekend to see him. Chocolate cake, said Frank. Maybe not chocolate cake, Ursula said, he's already eating so much chocolate.

And when, not right away but still only three weeks later, he was accepted into the protocol for the new drug, which took considerable behind-the-scenes lobbying with the doctors, he talked less about being ill, according to Donny, which seemed like a good sign, Kate felt, a sign that he was not feeling like a victim, feeling not that he *had* a disease but, rather, was living *with* a disease (that was the right cliché, wasn't it?), a more hospitable arrangement, said Jan, a kind of cohabitation which implied that it was something temporary, that it could be terminated, but terminated how, said Hilda, and when you say hospitable, Jan, I hear hospital. And it was encouraging, Stephen insisted, that from the start, at least from the time he was finally persuaded to make the telephone call to his doctor, he was willing to say the name of the disease, pronounce it often and easily, as if it were just another word, like boy or gallery or cigarette or money or deal, as in no big deal, Paolo interjected, because, as Stephen continued, to utter the name is a sign of health, a sign that one has accepted being who one is, mortal, vulnerable, not exempt, not an exception after all, it's a sign that one is willing, truly willing, to fight for one's life. And we must say the name, too, and often, Tanya added, we mustn't lag behind him in honesty, or let him feel that, the effort of honesty having been made, it's something done with and he can go on to other things. One is so much better prepared to help him, Wesley replied. In a way he's fortunate, said Yvonne, who had taken care of a problem at the New York store and was flying back to London this evening, sure, fortunate, said Wesley, no one is shunning him, Yvonne went on, no one's afraid to hug him or kiss him lightly on the mouth, in London we are, as usual, a few years behind you, people I know, people who would seem to be not even remotely at risk, are just terrified, but I'm impressed by how cool and rational you all are; you find us cool, asked Quentin. But I have to say, he's reported to have said, I'm terrified, I find it very hard to read (and you know how he loves to read, said Greg; yes, reading is his television, said Paolo) or to think, but I don't feel hysterical. I feel quite hysterical, Lewis said to Yvonne. But you're able to *do* something for him, that's wonderful, how I wish I could stay longer, Yvonne answered, it's rather beautiful, I can't help thinking, this utopia of friendship you've assembled around him (this pathetic utopia, said Kate), so that the disease, Yvonne concluded, is not, any more, out there. Yes, don't you think we're more at home here, with him, with the disease, said Tanya, because the imagined disease is so much worse than the reality of him, whom we all love, each in our fashion, having it. I know for me his getting it has quite demystified the disease, said Jan, I don't feel afraid, spooked, as I did before he became ill, when it was only news about remote acquaintances, whom I never saw again after they became ill. But you know you're not going to come down with the disease, Quentin said, to which Ellen replied, on her behalf, that's not the point, and possibly untrue, my gynaecologist says that everyone is at risk, everyone who has a sexual life, because sexuality is a chain that links each of us to many others, unknown others, and now the great chain of being has become a chain of death as well. It's not the same for you, Quentin insisted, it's not the same for you as it is for me or Lewis or Frank or Paolo or Max, I'm more and more frightened, and I have every reason to be. I don't think about whether I'm at risk or not, said Hilda, I know that I was afraid to know someone with the disease, afraid of what I'd see, what I'd feel, and after the first day I came to the hospital I felt so relieved. I'll never feel that way, that fear, again; he doesn't seem different from me. He's not, Quentin said.

According to Lewis, he talked more often about those who visited more often, which is natural, said Betsy, I think he's even keeping a tally. And among those who came or checked in by phone every day, the inner circle as it were, those who were getting more points, there was still a further competition, which was what was getting on Betsy's nerves, she confessed to Jan; there's always that vulgar jockeying for position around the bedside of the gravely ill, and though we all feel suffused with virtue at our loyalty to him (speak for yourself, said Jan), to the extent that we're carving time out of every day, or almost every day, though some of us are dropping out, as Xavier pointed out, aren't we getting at least as much out of this as he is. Are we, said Jan. We're rivals for a sign from him of special pleasure over a visit, each stretching for the brass ring of his favour, wanting to feel the most wanted, the true nearest and dearest, which is inevitable with someone who doesn't have a spouse and children or an official in-house lover, hierarchies that no one would dare contest, Betsy went on, so we are the family he's founded, without meaning to, without official titles and ranks (we, we, snarled Quentin); and is it so clear, though some of us, Lewis and Quentin and Tanya and Paolo, among others, are ex-lovers and all of us more or less than friends, which one of us he prefers, Victor said (now it's us, raged Quentin), because sometimes I think he looks forward

more to seeing Aileen, who has visited only three times, twice at the hospital and once since he's been home, than he does you or me; but, according to Tanya, after being very disappointed that Aileen hadn't come, now he was angry, while, according to Xavier, he was not really hurt but touchingly passive, accepting Aileen's absence as something he somehow deserved. But he's happy to have people around, said Lewis; he says when he doesn't have company he gets very sleepy, he sleeps (according to Quentin), and then perks up when someone arrives, it's important that he not feel ever alone. But, said Victor, there's one person he hasn't heard from, whom he'd probably like to hear from more than most of us; but she didn't just vanish, even right after she broke away from him, and he knows exactly where she lives now, said Kate, he told me he put in a call to her last Christmas Eve, and she said it's nice to hear from you and Merry Christmas, and he was shattered, according to Orson, and furious and disdainful, according to Ellen (what do you expect of her, said Wesley, she was burned out), but Kate wondered if maybe he hadn't phoned Nora in the middle of a sleepless night, what's the time difference, and Quentin said no, I don't think so, I think he wouldn't want her to know.

And when he was feeling even better and had regained the pounds he'd shed right away in the hospital, though the refrigerator started to fill up with organic wheat germ and grapefruit and skimmed milk (he's worried about his cholesterol count, Stephen lamented), and told Quentin he could manage by himself now, and did, he started asking everyone who visited how he looked, and everyone said he looked great, so much better than a few weeks ago, which didn't jibe with what anyone had told him at that time; but then it was getting harder and harder to know how he looked, to answer such a question honestly when among themselves they wanted to be honest, both for honesty's sake and (as Donny thought) to prepare for the worst, because he'd been looking like *this* for so long, at least it seemed so long, that it was as if he'd always been like this, how did he look before, but it was only a few months, and those words, pale and wan-looking and fragile, hadn't they always applied? And one Thursday Ellen, meeting Lewis at the door of the building, said, as they rode up together in the elevator, how is he *really*? But you see how he is, Lewis said tartly, he's fine, he's perfectly healthy, and Ellen understood that of course Lewis didn't think he was perfectly healthy but that he wasn't worse, and that was true, but wasn't it, well, almost heartless to talk like that. Seems inoffensive to me, Quentin said, but I know what you mean, I remember once talking to Frank, somebody, after all, who has volunteered to do five hours a week of office work at the Crisis Center (I know, said Ellen), and Frank was going on about this guy, diagnosed almost a year ago, and so much further along, who'd been complaining to Frank on the phone about the indifference of some doctor, and had gotten quite abusive about the doctor, and Frank was saying there was no reason to be so upset, the implication being that *he*, Frank, wouldn't behave so irrationally, and I said, barely able to control my scorn, but Frank, Frank, he has every reason to be upset, he's dying, and Frank said, said according to Quentin, oh, I don't like to think about it that way.

And it was while he was still home, recuperating, getting his weekly

treatment, still not able to do much work, he complained, but, according to Quentin, up and about most of the time and turning up at the office several days a week, that bad news came about two remote acquaintances, one in Houston and one in Paris, news that was intercepted by Quentin on the ground that it could only depress him, but Stephen contended that it was wrong to lie to him, it was so important for him to live in the truth; that had been one of his first victories, that he was candid, that he was even willing to crack jokes about the disease, but Ellen said it wasn't good to give him this end-of-the-world feeling, too many people were getting ill, it was becoming such a common destiny that maybe some of the will to fight for his life would be drained out of him if it seemed to be as natural as, well, death. Oh, Hilda said, who didn't know personally either the one in Houston or the one in Paris, but knew *of* the one in Paris, a pianist who specialized in twentieth-century Czech and Polish music, I have his records, he's such a valuable person, and, when Kate glared at her, continued defensively, I know every life is equally sacred, but that *is* a thought, another thought, I mean, all these valuable people who aren't going to have their normal four score as it is now, these people aren't going to be replaced, and it's such a loss to the culture. But this isn't going to go on for ever, Wesley said, it can't, they're bound to come up with something (they, they, muttered Stephen), but did you ever think, Greg said, that if some people don't die, I mean even if they can keep them alive (they, they, muttered Kate), they continue to be carriers, and that means, if you have a conscience, that you can never make love, make love fully, as you'd been wont – wantonly, Ira said – to do. But it's better than dying, said Frank. And in all his talk about the future, when he allowed himself to be hopeful, according to Quentin, he never mentioned the prospect that even if he didn't die, if he were so fortunate as to be among the first generation of the disease's survivors, never mentioned, Kate confirmed, that whatever happened it was over, the way he had lived until now, but, according to Ira, he did think about it, the end of bravado, the end of folly, the end of trusting life, the end of taking life for granted, and of treating life as something that, samurai-like, he thought himself ready to throw away lightly, impudently; and Kate recalled, sighing, a brief exchange she'd insisted on having as long as two years ago, huddling on a banquette covered with steel-grey industrial carpet on an upper level of The Prophet and toking up for their next foray on to the dance floor: she'd said hesitantly, for it felt foolish asking a prince of debauchery to, well, take it easy, and she wasn't keen on playing big sister, a role, as Hilda confirmed, he inspired in many women, are you being careful, honey, you know what I mean. And he replied, Kate went on, no, I'm not, listen, I can't, I just can't, sex is too important to me, always has been (he started talking like that, according to Victor, after Nora left him), and if I get it, well, I get it. But he wouldn't talk like that now, would he, said Greg; he must feel awfully foolish now, said Betsy, like someone who went on smoking, saying I can't give up cigarettes, but when the bad X-ray is taken even the most besotted nicotine addict can stop on a dime. But sex isn't like cigarettes, is it, said Frank, and, besides, what good does it do to remember that he was reckless, said Lewis angrily, the appalling thing is that you just have to be unlucky once, and wouldn't he feel even worse if he'd stopped three years ago and had come down with it anyway, since one of the most terrifying features of the disease is that you don't know when you contracted it, it could have been ten years ago, because surely this disease has existed for years and years, long before it was recognized; that is, named. Who knows how long (I think a lot about that, said Max) and who knows (I know what you're going to say, Stephen interrupted) how many are going to get it.

I'm feeling fine, he's reported to have said whenever someone asked him how he was, which was almost always the first question anyone asked. Or: I'm feeling better, how are you? But he said other things, too. I'm playing leapfrog with myself, he is reported to have said, according to Victor. And. There must be a way to get something positive out of this situation, he's reported to have said to Kate. How American of him, said Paolo. Well, said Betsy, you know the old American adage: When you've got a lemon, make lemonade. The one thing I'm sure I couldn't take, Jan said he said to her, is becoming disfigured, but Stephen hastened to point out the disease doesn't take that form very often any more, its profile is mutating, and, in conversation with Ellen, wheeled up words like blood-brain barrier; I never thought there was a barrier *there*, said Jan. But he mustn't know about Max, Ellen said, that would really depress him, please don't tell him, he'll have to know, Quentin said grimly, and he'll be furious not to have been told. But there's time for that, when they take Max off the respirator, said Ellen; but isn't it incredible, Frank said, Max was fine, not feeling ill at all, and then to wake up with a fever of a hundred and five, unable to breathe, but that's the way it often starts, with absolutely no warning, Stephen said, the disease has so many forms. And when, after another week had gone by, he asked Quentin where Max was, he didn't question Quentin's account of a spree in the Bahamas, but then the number of people who visited regularly was thinning out, partly because the old feuds that had been put aside through the first hospitalization and the return home had resurfaced, and the flickering enmity between Lewis and Frank exploded, even though Kate did her best to mediate between them, and also because he himself had done something to loosen the bonds of love that united the friends around him, by seeming to take them all for granted, as if it were perfectly normal for so many people to carve out so much time and attention for him, visit him every few days, talk about him incessantly on the phone with each other; but, according to Paolo, it wasn't that he was less grateful, it was just something he was getting used to, the visits. It had become, with time, a more ordinary kind of situation, a kind of ongoing party, first at the hospital and now since he was home, barely on his feet again, it being clear, said Robert, that I'm on the B list; but Kate said, that's absurd, there's no list; and Victor said, but there is, only it's not he, it's Quentin who's drawing it up. He wants to see us, we're helping him, we have to do it the way he wants, he fell down yesterday on the way to the bathroom, he mustn't be told about Max (but he already knew, according to Donny), it's getting worse.

When I was home, he is reported to have said, I was afraid to sleep, as I was dropping off each night it felt like just that, as if I were falling down a black hole, to sleep felt like giving in to death, I slept every night with the light on; but here, in the hospital, I'm less afraid. And to Quentin he said, one morning, the fear rips through me, it tears me open; and, to Ira, it presses me together, squeezes me toward myself. Fear gives everything its hue, its high. I feel so, I don't know how to say it, exalted, he said to Quentin. Calamity is an amazing high, too. Sometimes I feel *so* well, so powerful, it's as if I could jump out of my skin. Am I going crazy, or what? Is it all this attention and coddling I'm getting from everybody, like a child's dream of being loved? Is it the drugs? I know it sounds crazy but sometimes I think this is a *fantastic* experience, he said shyly; but there was also the bad taste in the mouth, the pressure in the head and at the back of the neck, the red, bleeding gums, the painful, if pink-lobed, breathing, and his ivory pallor, colour of white chocolate. Among those who wept when told over the phone that he was back in the hospital were Kate and Stephen (who'd been called by Quentin), and Ellen, Victor, Aileen, and Lewis (who were called by Kate), and Xavier and Ursula (who were called by Stephen). Among those who didn't weep were Hilda, who said that she'd just learned that her seventy-five-year-old aunt was dying of the disease, which she'd contracted from a transfusion given during her successful double bypass of five years ago, and Frank and Donny and Betsy, but this didn't mean, according to Tanya, that they weren't moved and appalled, and Quentin thought they might not be coming soon to the hospital but would send presents; the room, he was in a private room this time, was filling up with flowers, and plants, and books, and tapes. The high tide of barely suppressed acrimony of the last weeks at home subsided into the routines of hospital visiting, though more than a few resented Quentin's having charge of the visiting book (but it was Quentin who had the idea, Lewis pointed out); now, to insure a steady stream of visitors, preferably no more than two at a time (this, the rule in all hospitals, wasn't enforced here, at least on his floor; whether out of kindness or inefficiency, no one could decide), Quentin had to be called first, to get one's time slot, there was no more casual dropping by. And his mother could no longer be prevented from taking a plane and installing herself in a hotel near the hospital; but he seemed to mind her daily presence less than expected, Quentin said; said Ellen it's we who mind, do you suppose she'll stay long. It was easier to be generous with each other visiting him here in the hospital, as Donny pointed out, than at home, where one minded never being alone with him; coming here, in our twos and twos, there's no doubt about what our role is, how we should be, collective, funny, distracting, undemanding, light, it's important to be light, for in all this dread there is gaiety, too, as the poet said, said Kate. (His eyes, his glittering eyes, said Lewis.) His eyes looked dull, extinguished, Wesley said to Xavier, but Betsy said his face, not just his eyes, looked soulful, warm; whatever is there, said Kate, I've never been so aware of his eyes; and Stephen said, I'm afraid of what my eyes show, the way I watch him, with too much intensity, or a phony kind of casualness, said Victor. And, unlike at home, he was clean-shaven each morning, at whatever hour they visited him; his curly hair was always combed; but he complained that the nurses had changed since he was here the last time, and that he didn't like the change, he wanted everyone to be the same. The room was furnished now with some of his personal effects (odd word for one's things, said Ellen), and Tanya brought drawings and a letter from her nine-year-old dyslexic son, who was writing now, since she'd purchased a computer; and Donny brought champagne and some helium balloons, which were anchored to the foot of his bed; tell me about something that's

going on, he said, waking up from a nap to find Donny and Kate at the side of his bed, beaming at him; tell me a story, he said wistfully, said Donny, who couldn't think of anything to say; *you're* the story, Kate said. And Xavier brought an eighteenth-century Guatemalan wooden statue of St Sebastian with upcast eyes and open mouth, and when Tanya said what's that, a tribute to eros past, Xavier said where I come from Sebastian is venerated as a protector against pestilence. Pestilence symbolized by arrows? Symbolized by arrows. All people remember is the body of a beautiful youth bound to a tree, pierced by arrows (of which he always seems oblivious, Tanya interjected), people forget that the story continues, Xavier continued, that when the Christian women came to bury the martyr they found him still alive and nursed him back to health. And he said, according to Stephen, I didn't know St Sebastian didn't die. It's undeniable, isn't it, said Kate on the phone to Stephen, the fascination of the dying. It makes me ashamed. We're learning how to die, said Hilda, I'm not ready to learn, said Aileen; and Lewis, who was coming straight from the other hospital, the hospital where Max was still being kept in I.C.U., met Tanya getting out of the elevator on the tenth floor, and as they walked together down the shiny corridor past the open doors, averting their eyes from the other patients sunk in their beds, with tubes in their noses, irradiated by the bluish light from the television sets, the thing I can't bear to think about, Tanya said to Lewis, is someone dying with the TV on.

He has that strange, unnerving detachment now, said Ellen, that's what upsets me, even though it makes it easier to be with him. Sometimes he was querulous. I can't stand them coming in here taking my blood every morning, what are they doing with all that blood, he is reported to have said; but where was his anger, Jan wondered. Mostly he was lovely to be with, always saying how are *you*, how are you feeling. He's so sweet now, said Aileen. He's so nice, said Tanya. (Nice, nice, groaned Paolo.) At first he was very ill, but he was rallying, according to Stephen's best information, there was no fear of his not recovering this time, and the doctor spoke of his being discharged from the hospital in another ten days if all went well, and the mother was persuaded to fly back to Mississippi, and Quentin was readying the penthouse for his return. And he was still writing his diary, not showing it to anyone, though Tanya, first to arrive one late-winter morning, and finding him dozing, peeked, and was horrified, according to Greg, not by anything she read but by a progressive change in his handwriting: in the recent pages, it was becoming spidery, less legible, and some lines of script wandered and tilted about the page. I was thinking, Ursula said to Quentin, that the difference between a story and a painting or photograph is that in a story you can write, He's still alive. But in a painting or a photo you can't show 'still'. You can just show him being alive. He's still alive, Stephen said.

PICTURES

1

in touch
checking in

2

as you'd been wont – wantonly
wantonly
eros past

3

the hospital room was choked with flowers
everybody likes flowers
surplus flowers
the room . . . was filling up with flowers

4

but he did stop smoking
he didn't miss cigarettes at all

ENDPAPERS

Fear gives everything its hue, its high

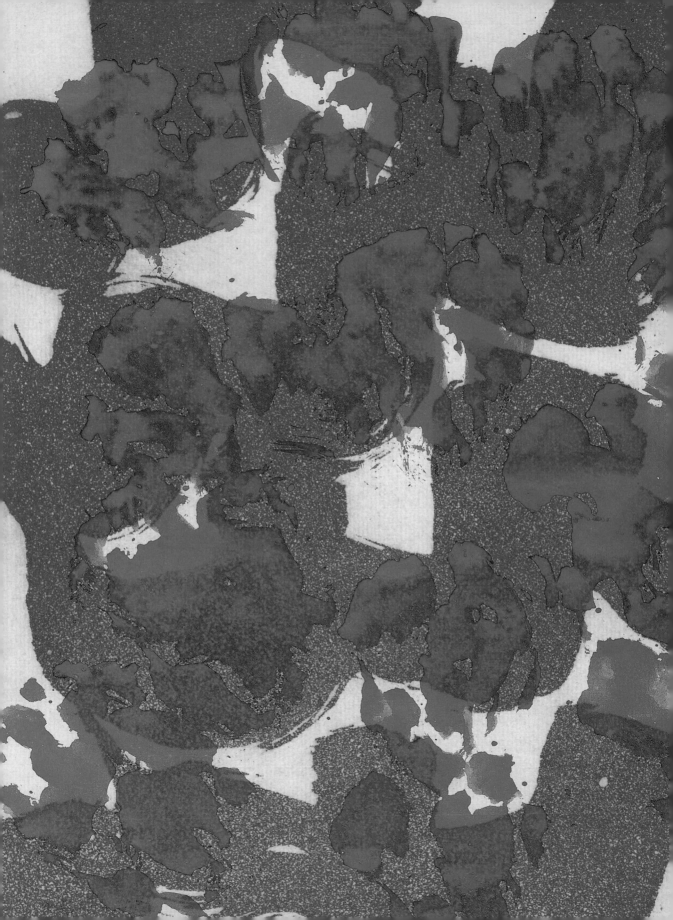